Bible Critters

BUGS!

Zonder**kidz**

Zonder**kidz**®

The children's group of Zondervan

www.zonderkidz.com

Bible Critters: Bugs
Copyright © 2002 by Pat Matuszak
Illustrations copyright © 2002 by David Sheldon

Requests for information should be addressed to:
Zonderkidz, Grand Rapids, Michigan 49530

ISBN: 0-310-70811-7

Editor: Gwen Ellis
Interior Design: Michelle Lenger

Printed in China
06 07 08 09 • 6 5 4 3 2

Written by **Pat Matuszak**

Illustrated by **David Sheldon**

To my bug-loving sons, John and Pete.
Thanks for teaching me to treasure the
little things!
P.M.

for Tini
D.S.

In a palace in the desert
Lived a king who had a pet—
The strangest creeping creature
That you have ever met!

His pet was not a dog or cat
Or all those common things.
He was a shiny beetle bug
With horns and whirring wings.

King Pharaoh called him Scarab
And wore him in his hair!
He fed him from the table.
Gave people quite a scare!

He'd smile like he was being nice
and say, "Here have some cream."
But when they poured the pitcher,
Scarab bug would make them scream.

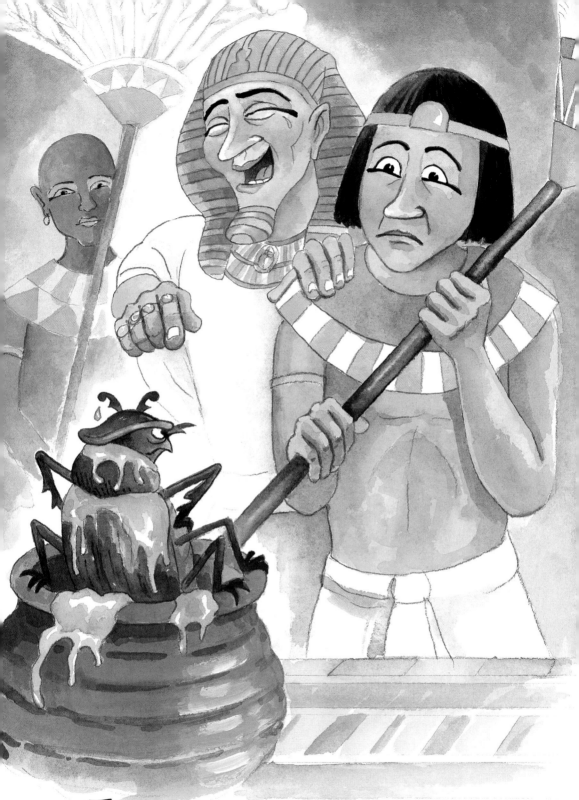

The little beetle liked these games
'Til he hid in the honey—
When his wings got stuck together
Then he knew it wasn't funny.

One day a man named Moses
Came to the King to say
That God had said to free his slaves
And Pharaoh must obey.

Old Pharaoh was too busy
To listen to that plea,
So God caused stuff to happen
To make his hard eyes see.

First frogs came hopping from the Nile
Whose water turned blood red.
They croaked on every windowsill
And hopped on Pharaoh's bed.

They fell into the bread dough
And scared the royal bakers.
They looked like floods of moving eyes
That filled all Egypt's acres.

Around the royal palace,
Swarmed clouds of gnats like rain.
They flew in Pharaoh's ears and face.
They really were a pain!

The horses didn't like them.
They swished their tails for hours,
But the gnats just kept on coming,
Raining down like summer showers.

One day outside the window,
Pharaoh heard a buzzing sound.
Then clouds of hairy, red-eyed flies
Filled all the sky and ground.

Brave Moses tried to warn the king
Those ugly bugs were coming,
But the king called in his drummers
To drown out all their humming.

Those flies, they landed everywhere.
They sat upon the food.
Then Pharaoh yelled and told the crowd,
"I'm in an awful mood."

The flies were in the soup bowls.
The flies were on their hats.
They buzzed around and filled the air.
They even scared the cats.

But every time that Moses came
Again to warn the king,
Pharaoh laughed or looked away—
He wouldn't do a thing!

Then he heard a splat-plop-swoosh
Outside the window pane—
And a gang of big green locust
Came down like falling rain.

Oh my, those bugs were hungry!
They chewed up every tree,
'Cause Pharaoh didn't lift a hand
To set God's people free.

The streets were very slippery
With gobs of bright green goo,
So the shoemaker invented
A locust-squashing shoe!

When Pharaoh went out riding
In his carriage with gold lace,
He kept the curtains closed so tight
The bugs weren't in his face.

Those locust would have flown away
In just about a second,
If Pharaoh had just heard God's word
And with it he had reckoned.

What could a man like Moses do
To get a king to see
That if he didn't hear God's voice,
The worst was yet to be?

Moses kept on knocking–
Back to Pharaoh's house he'd go.
But every time he warned him,
That stubborn king said "No!"

Hail, darkness, and a plague
Would come on Egypt land,
And all because the king would not
Allow what God had planned.

Back and forth poor Moses came
With messages so clear.
The king would need to change his mind
Or give up all that's dear.

But bit-by-bug, God's word got through
King Pharaoh's heart of stone—
He set God's people free at once
With orders from his throne.

Creepy, crawly bugs and frogs
Had helped a king to hear!
The words that Moses brought from God
Had made the whole thing clear.

You can read the whole, true story of the Bible bugs and Moses in your Bible.

Just look up Exodus 8:1—10:29

Scarab

The Egyptians believed the scarab was a symbol for eternal life. Rings and seals with the scarab beetle imprint were used by royalty.

The scarab beetle lays its eggs in balls of dung and is strong enough to roll dirt balls to protected places where the eggs will hatch safely.

Beetles have shiny, hard covers that protect their wings like armor when they are not flying. They come in all sorts of colors and spots. Some even have horns on their heads.

Flies

Flies see the world through thousands of tiny eyes. They can see behind them without turning their heads, which is what makes it so hard to swat a fly! Whenever flies come in big groups called swarms, it means something is terribly wrong. They often lay eggs in dead animals, so many flies can mean many fish or cattle have died from disease or lack of water. They bring disease to healthy animals and people from the dead animals they grew in. God sent flies to warn Pharaoh that something evil was going on in Egypt. The Bible says the biting flies were so thick that they covered people, animals, and houses.

Locust

Locust are the best jumpers in the insect kingdom and they can also fly. They have chewing jaws, are always hungry, and spit out green "locust tobacco juice" after they chew plants. When they gather in large groups or swarms, they can eat up all the green leaves and grass. But their damage isn't over when they run out of food and move on to the next place, they lay eggs in the ground near the roots of trees. Slimy baby larvae hatch and eat up the trees' roots. Locust were sent by God to try to change the Egyptian king's mind about letting the Hebrew slaves go free.

Although locust could be a pest because they ate the farmers' crops, some people turned the tables on the locust and ate them as food!

*R*ead Matthew 3:4 and Mark 1:6 to find out which Bible character ate locust with honey topping!